When Grandma Almost Fell Off the Mountain

& Other Stories

by Barbara Ann Porte

pictures by Maxie Chambliss

Orchard Books   New York

Orchard Books, 95 Madison Avenue, New York, NY 10016

Manufactured in the United States of America. Printed by Barton Press, Inc.
Bound by Horowitz/Rae. Book design by Mina Greenstein.
The text of this book is set in 14 point ITC Clearface Regular. The illustrations are colored pencil and
watercolor reproduced in full color.   10   9   8   7   6   5   4   3   2   1

Library of Congress Cataloging-in-Publication Data
Porte, Barbara Ann. When Grandma almost fell off the mountain and other stories / by Barbara Ann
Porte ; pictures by Maxie Chambliss.   p.   cm. "A Richard Jackson book."
Summary: Grandma tells surprising and unusual stories about a vacation she took with her family when
she was a little girl.
ISBN 0-531-05965-0.   ISBN 0-531-08565-1 (lib. bdg.)
[1. Vacations—Fiction.   2. Grandmothers—Fiction.   3. Family life—Fiction.]   I. Chambliss, Maxie, ill.
II. Title.   PZ7.P7995Wh   1993   [E]—dc20   91-41174

For my grandparents,
Dora Luboff and Samuel Porte,
Rebecca Karp and William Spodak,
and for Zachary Ryan Alberico,
their great-great-grandson

—B.A.P.

For Eleanor Mae Pitts
and her little Ford roadster

—M.C.

$\mathbf{T}$he day Stella and Zelda visited their grandma and asked her to tell them a story, she said, "I don't know stories, but I'll tell you about the time my sister and I went to Florida by car with our parents. Our grandparents lived there. It was summer vacation. Our grandmother who lived with us came along for the ride. That was some trip, believe me. I stood all the way."

"Stood?" asked Zelda.

"Yes," said her grandma. "We had a very big car. Most cars were big in those days, but this car was big even for then. It was a black La Salle with running boards. It had a very loud horn that sometimes honked by itself in the middle of the night.

Then my father, your great-grandfather, would pull his overcoat on over his pajamas and run outside to try and make it stop. Sometimes it did and sometimes it didn't. Either way, the neighbors complained in the morning. 'Not getting enough sleep will make even grown-up people cranky,' our mother told us, a bit cranky herself the next day."

"That's all very interesting," said Stella, "but why did you stand?"

"So I could see out the window," her grandmother said. "Sitting, I'd be too short. I stood on the floor in the back and held on to the strap."

"What strap?" Zelda asked.

"Cars came with straps in those days. No one knew why. My grandmother used hers to hoist herself in and out of the car. She was over eighty and hardly taller than my sister. I held on to mine so I wouldn't fall. I saw a lot that way, believe me."

"What did you see?" asked Stella.

"Cows," said her grandma. "Horses and sheep, chickens and geese, sometimes a mule. Once we saw a bear by the roadside, holding a sign. He was standing in front of a traveling show, waving in customers. We saw acres of wheat. That was awful."

"Awful how?" Zelda asked.

"We drove past miles and miles of it. My eyes squinched shut. My face puffed up. I could hardly breathe. 'It looks as if Clarissa's allergic to wheat,' my mother said, speaking from experience. She was correct. I was fine by the time we left the wheat fields behind and stopped to pick cotton."

"You picked cotton?" asked Stella.

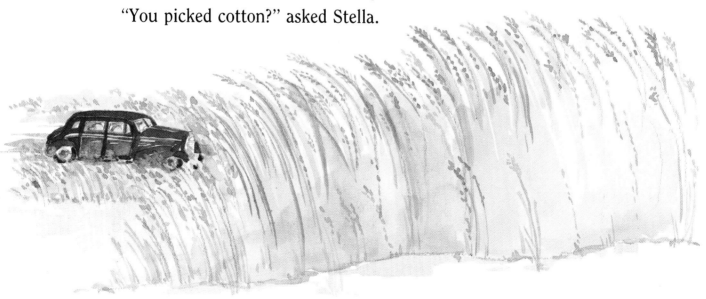

"Our father did. Using his pocketknife, he cut off one sprig. Unfortunately, just at that exact minute the farmer whose cotton it was came by on his tractor and stopped. 'You want to buy some of my cotton?' he asked. Of course our father didn't. 'No, thank you,' he said. 'I was only showing my girls how cotton looks when it blooms.' The farmer frowned. 'I see,' he said. 'If everybody passing by did that, I'd have no cotton left to pick come picking time.' Then he turned his tractor back on and drove off. Our father got back into our car and drove off himself.

" 'See, that farmer was right,' he said when we'd gone a few miles. We still had miles ahead of us to go."

"Did you get bored?" Zelda wanted to know.

"Bored? I should say not," said her grandmother. "My sister and I kept our eyes peeled, believe me."

"For what?" asked both girls.

"Who knew? Anything was possible," their grandmother said. "Highways weren't what they are now. There were just two lanes most of the way, sometimes four. They wound through every bitty town. We stopped a lot, now and then to let a pig cross the road, sometimes for tourist attractions. Once we stopped to see a tankful of snapping turtles eat watermelon rinds. Every afternoon we pulled off the road for ice cream. That was how my sister fell into a lily pad pond on her swing."

Stella and Zelda looked at each other and rolled their eyes.

"I'm only telling you what happened," said their grandma. "I wouldn't make up such a story. The ice cream stand was next to a playground. The playground was next to a pond. After my sister and I had eaten our ice cream, we went to play on the swings. My mother pushed me on one, and Claudia swung herself on the other. She had just learned to pump. She pumped and pumped. 'I think that's high enough,' our mother said. But it was already too late. The words were no sooner out of her mouth than the seat of Claudia's swing broke away from the chains and flew through the air with Claudia still on it. Fortunately, it landed in the water."

"Did your sister know how to swim?" Zelda asked.

"Not at all," her grandma said. "Luckily, our grandmother was close by and saw what had happened."

"Could your grandmother swim?" Zelda asked.

"Not swim. She shouted. 'Stand up, Claudia,' she shouted, over and over. Finally Claudia did. She was covered with mud, and lily leaves hung from her hair, but the water came up only to her waist. See, it was deep enough to break her fall, but not to drown her. She did have a sore back, a stiff neck, and black-and-blue marks all over for most of the rest of the trip.

" 'Such beautiful girls,' our grandparents said when we arrived. Then they asked, 'Why is the older one limping?' Our mother explained. 'She had a bit of an accident swimming,' she said. Our grandmother rubbed liniment on Claudia's back. It came in a jar and was black. It stained her clothes and smelled awful. 'It will make you feel much better, though,' our grandmother told her. 'I'm all better *now*,' Claudia said the next morning. She meant she didn't need any more treatment."

"Did all five of you stay with your grandparents, or did you go to a hotel?" Both girls wanted to know.

"Yes," said their grandmother.

"Yes, which?" They sounded a teensy bit exasperated for such nice children.

"Yes, both," said their grandmother. "Aren't you girls listening? We stayed with our grandparents in the hotel where they lived. They had a penthouse apartment with a rooftop garden. Our grandfather grew orchids and roses there, also rhubarb and tomatoes. 'I used to keep a rabbit, but it got to be too much trouble,' he told us. It was our uncle's hotel, but our grandparents ran it."

"What did your uncle do?" asked the girls.

"We asked that, too," said their grandma. "No one knew, but whatever it was, he was quite well-to-do, and very good-looking. He was straight-backed and slim, with black wavy hair and dark eyes that went through you. He had a drooping mustache and a dazzling smile. He was a bachelor still, and paid a lot of attention to us while we were there."

"What was his name?" Stella asked.

"Ezekiel," said her grandmother. "Well, that was his real name, but no one called him that. Everybody called him John, except for his parents. They called him by his middle name, Sasha, after *his* grandfather."

Zelda sighed. "If his name was Ezekiel, why did everybody call him John? Why didn't they call him Zeke?" she asked.

"That's a good question," said her grandmother. "It's exactly what I asked my father. This was what he told me. When Ezekiel was small, he didn't speak too clearly. His first day of school, the teacher couldn't understand him. 'What is your name?' she asked. 'Speak up, please. I don't know what you are saying. Never mind,' she said at last. 'I'll just call you John.' That's what she did. She also wrote it in her roll book. By the end of the first week it had caught on. Our uncle didn't mind. 'Why would he have?' our father asked. 'John was such an easy name to say, and also to spell.' "

"Did you and your sister enjoy your visit?" Stella asked.

"Oh, yes," said her grandmother. "At least for the most part. Now and then we had a bad experience. Eating out, for instance, was once almost a disaster. Claudia blamed our mother."

"Your mother? What did she do?" asked Stella.

"She didn't *do* anything," her grandma answered. "Claudia only meant it was because of her we were eating out in the first place. Usually we ate in the dining room of our uncle's hotel. The food was excellent, and so was the service. But almost every night our mother said, 'At least once in a while, while we're here, it would be nice to eat out in a restaurant.' Well, of course we were already eating in a restaurant, but our mother meant in someone else's restaurant. She wanted to get all dressed up and drive to someplace posh with a canopy at the entrance and a doorman. 'A person on vacation wants a bit of atmosphere,' she said. Probably she also wanted air-conditioning. Our uncle's hotel just had fans.

"That was how it happened one night our father
borrowed our uncle's limousine and his chauffeur,
and Claudia and I and our parents rode in it to a famous
restaurant with fountains in front and flamingos, also
a canopy and a doorman. Inside were marble floors,
mirrored walls, and elaborate chandeliers. It was also
very cold.

" 'We have reservations,' our father informed the maitre d',
who showed us to a round table with a pink tablecloth, flowers,
and candles. A waiter brought us drinks in long-stemmed
goblets. Claudia's and mine were ginger ale, each with a
maraschino cherry and crushed ice. We pretended we were
grown up. 'Such well-mannered girls,' the waiter said. So did
the maitre d'. 'Thank you,' our parents said. Even so, we had to
leave early. It was Claudia's fault."

"What did *she* do?" Zelda asked.

"Didn't do," said her grandmother. "She didn't listen. Along one wall in the restaurant was a display of sculptured ice, large multicolored pieces carved to look like animals. 'Why don't you girls go have a look?' our father said. That's what we did. When we had nearly reached the end, we saw two large blocks of uncut ice, blue on top of green. 'You can touch the blue but not the green,' we overheard some father tell his child. Probably there was a sign, but we didn't see it. 'He's not my father. I don't have to listen,' Claudia said, and reaching out one hand, she touched the green. Then she screamed. That was how we learned about dry ice, and that something so cold still can burn.

The chef came running from the kitchen, holding out a ladle full of melted butter. 'Butter's good for burns,' he said. He buttered Claudia's hand. We hurried home. 'Butter's no good.

It's just an old folktale,'
our grandfather said. He
got out a jar of yellow salve.

'Burn salve,' he told us, and smeared it on top of
the butter. 'Now you'll be fine,' he told Claudia. He sat her on
his lap and rocked her. That's when she stopped crying.
Afterward, whenever our parents went out for dinner, they left
Claudia and me behind. We didn't mind. We ate scrumptious
desserts with all three of our grandparents, and listened to their
conversation."

"What did they talk about?" Stella asked, yawning.
"Who remembers? It was a long time ago," her grandmother
answered. "I remember the desserts much better—seven-layer
chocolate cakes, Nesselrode pies, biscuit tortoni. Of course, the
day I almost drowned, that was all they talked about."
"You almost drowned!" The two girls gasped.

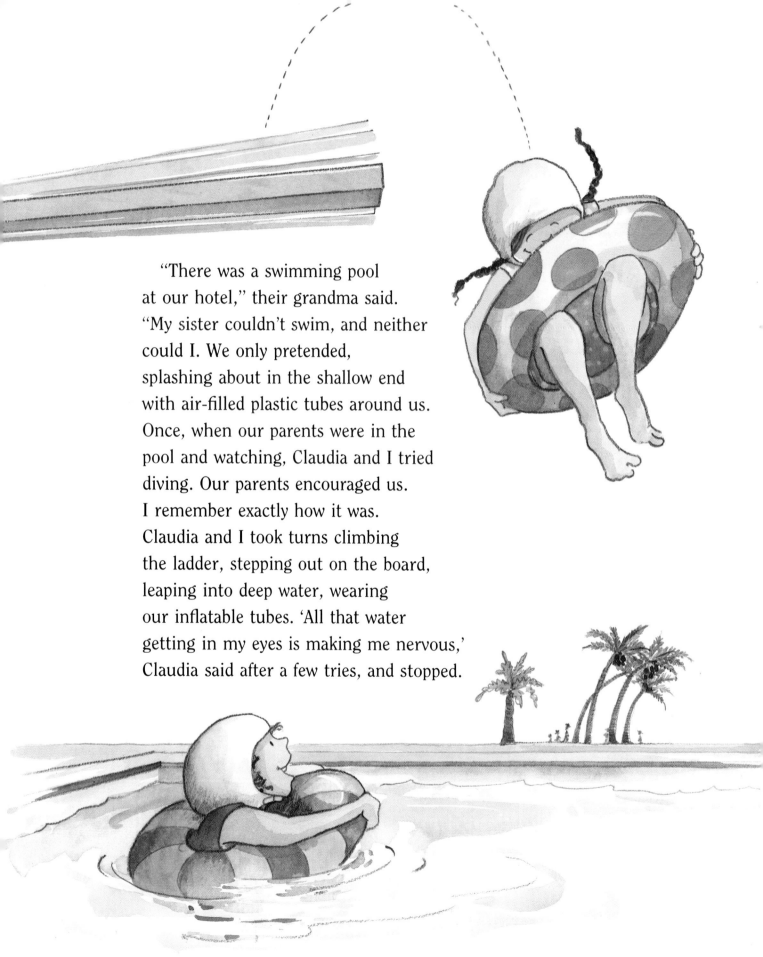

"There was a swimming pool at our hotel," their grandma said. "My sister couldn't swim, and neither could I. We only pretended, splashing about in the shallow end with air-filled plastic tubes around us. Once, when our parents were in the pool and watching, Claudia and I tried diving. Our parents encouraged us. I remember exactly how it was. Claudia and I took turns climbing the ladder, stepping out on the board, leaping into deep water, wearing our inflatable tubes. 'All that water getting in my eyes is making me nervous,' Claudia said after a few tries, and stopped.

"I kept going. I don't know whether it was thinking how much braver I was than my sister, or all that water in my eyes that made me so careless, but the last time I dived I didn't have on my tube. Either I'd forgotten it, or it had slipped off without my noticing. Naturally, when I hit the water, I went under. I came up gasping for air. I had only time enough to see my parents' horrified faces before I went under again. Fortunately, when I came up my second time, still sputtering, the lifeguard grabbed me, held me out, and hit me on my back. 'Thank you,' my parents said, as he handed me over. For the rest of that day, I sat beneath a coconut tree, next to my grandma from home, and kept her company. 'I worried all day,' Claudia told me later. 'I was afraid a coconut would fall off the tree and land on one of your heads.' "

"Then why didn't she warn you?" said Stella.

"Probably because in those days Claudia was forever being told she worried too much for no reason," her grandma answered. "I think she couldn't bear to hear one of our parents say again, 'Our Claudia is such a worrywart.'"

"I see," said Stella. Then she asked, "What else did you do in Florida besides eat in and swim?"

Stella and Zelda's grandma looked thoughtful. "Do?" she said in a while. "It was too hot to do too much of anything. I remember going to the beach to find seashells our first week there. The sand was so hot I burned the bottoms of my feet walking on it. My father picked me up and carried me, piggyback, down to the water to cool them. The next day he bought me a pair of wooden sandals. Wearing them, I could walk anywhere on the beach. Of course I didn't have to. We learned to stay in the shade during the hottest part of the day and collect seashells at night.

"Luckily for us, though, some days were cloudy. On one of them our uncle took us to the parrot jungle." Zelda and Stella's grandmother stopped talking and went into another room. She came back with a snapshot. "See, this is me in the parrot jungle," she said.

Both girls peered closely. They saw a picture in black-and-white of a little girl wearing shorts and a midriff. She was smiling at a parrot perched on her shoulder biting her barrette.

"That's really you? It doesn't look like you," Zelda said, squinting.

"Well, I was much younger then," said her grandmother.

"I think it looks a little like Grandma. She still has the same eyes," Stella said.

"Right," said her grandmother, and went on speaking. "Before we left the parrot jungle, we looked in the gift shop. 'You can each choose one thing,' our uncle told us. My sister chose a wooden back scratcher. I chose a paper fan. Hers lasted much longer, but I got more use out of mine. I waved it all the way home from Florida in the car. Cars in those days did not come with air-conditioners. We drove with all the windows open, singing. One day my sister and I sang 'Peter, Peter, Pumpkin Eater' ninety-nine times without stopping. 'You're driving me crazy,' our mother finally said, and gave us lunch early to keep us quiet."

"What else did you and your sister do on the way home?"
Zelda asked.

"To tell the truth, I remember only one other thing," said her
grandma. "That was the time we almost fell off the mountain in
our car in a rainstorm."

"But you didn't," said Stella.

"I know," said her grandmother. "But it was some downpour,
believe me. Taking the mountain route home was our father's
idea. 'There's nothing else to compare with the scenery,' he told
us. No doubt he was right, but it was hard just seeing the road
through the buckets of rain. 'I think we should pull over,' our
mother said. 'It's bound to let up soon,' our father said.

That was when the car went out of control. All four tires lost their grip, and two of them slipped a tiny bit over the edge of the mountain. 'It's a good thing I'm such a good driver,' our father said, recovering, then pulling off the road. 'It's a good thing I grabbed him,' said our grandmother, who was riding in back and had wrapped her arms around our father's neck. Afterward, she always believed it had been her quick action that day that had saved us. 'It's a good thing there were no cars behind you,' said our mother. 'We almost fell off the mountain,' my sister and I chanted gleefully. We thought it was by far the most exciting part of our trip. While we waited in the car for the rain to let up, our mother consulted her maps. She picked a new route. 'I'm sure mountain views are better, but I'd sooner see everyone home in one piece,' she said."

"Were you glad to get home?" Stella asked.

"Oh, yes," said her grandma. "The best part of almost any trip is coming home and telling all your friends and relatives about it. Of course, in our case, a lot of friends and relatives had questions. 'You did what?' some of them said. 'Who did you say this happened to?' asked others. 'Are you absolutely positive?' Some were quite persistent. 'Of course we are. We were there. It happened to us,' we had to say over and over."

"What did you do the summer after that? Did you all go back to Florida?" Zelda asked.

"We went to Canada instead," her grandmother answered. "Only our grandmother didn't go. 'One mountain was enough excitement for me,' she said. 'I think I'll stay home and keep an eye on the house. You can send me a postcard from Quebec.'

" 'Dear Grandma, it's very nice in Canada,' we wrote. 'People speak French in Quebec. There are a lot of lakes and rivers, also mountains. The weather is fine. It hasn't rained once since we left home, but our mother says it's too cool to go swimming. Nothing bad has happened yet. We miss you and wish you were here. Love, Claudia and Clarissa.' We sent a postcard to Florida, too, with a similar message. It was certainly true. Canada *was* nice, but we missed our relatives."

"Well, of course you did. We would have, too," Stella said.

"Really?" asked her grandmother.

"Really," Zelda said. "That's why we spend vacations with you."

Stella nodded.

Their grandma looked extremely pleased.